WITHI

BASTARD

Max de Radiguès

FANTAGRAPHICS BOOKS INC.
7563 Lake City Way NE
Seattle, Washington, 98115

www.fantagraphics.com

Editor and Associate Publisher: Eric Reynolds
Book Design: Sean David Williams
Production: Paul Baresh and RJ Casey
Publisher: Gary Groth

Bastard is copyright © 2018 Max de Radiguès. This edition is copyright © 2018 Fantagraphics Books Inc. Permission to reproduce content must be obtained from the author or publisher. All rights reserved.

Published with the support of the Wallonia-Brussels Federation.

ISBN 978-1-68396-130-7
Library of Congress Control Number: 2018936463

First printing: July 2018
Printed in Korea

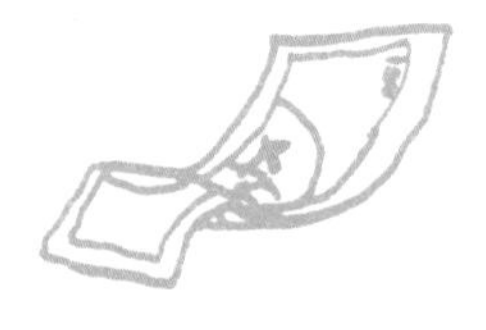

BASTARD

Max de Radiguès

FANTAGRAPHICS BOOKS
SEATTLE, WASHINGTON

Batavia Public Library
Batavia, Illinois

TACOS MEXICO

1$
TA
Quesadillas Supreme
Nachos Supreme

TACOS
Here.

Thanks, bye.

April?!

Is that really you?!

Haha! April?!

This is crazy! It's been what, 10? 15 years? Haha...

So what's up? You live around here?

I'm sorry, but you must be confusing me for someone else.

April! It's me, Mark!!!

You're mistaken. Sorry... Have a good day...

But...

MOTEL
Pony
MOTEL

We gotta move.
What?

Now?

Mhm.

PFFFF

We didn't even get to use the pool...

I ran into an old friend.
He recognized me.

April or May?
April...

Okay... I'll load the car and you check us out...

You'll be all right?
Yep.

Eugene.
NANCY

Cold tacos for lunch once we're on the road.
CLING

Meet you at the car in 10 minutes...
CLING

Yep.

28
RRRR

WHOA!

Can you check the map to see where we'll stop tonight?

Mhm.

AIR BAG
MAP

CLICK
Mmm.
According to the itinerary, we have...
Fuck...
What?
Checkpoint.

What do we do?

They're searching the cars!

CLICK
Okay...
You're having an asthma attack.
What?
Wait, what are we doing?!
Mom!
VRRR

Wha... What are you doing?!
Stop!

Don't worry, kitty...

VRRR

Uhh?

Ready?
Mhm.

Sorry officer, I need to get my son to the ER as fast as possible...

Asthma attack...

JERRY

Okay.

Is there a problem?

No problem, ma'am. My partner will escort you to the hospital...

Sorry? What?!

It's going to be okay... You don't need to do that...

It's our job, ma'am.
POLICE

Go ahead... Good luck...

Thanks. You're my hero!

Pfffrrr...
My hero!
Haha!
You should talk...
What was with that asthma attack you just had?
Looked more like epilepsy...
Stop it!
He could see you!
Haha!
Pff...

CAFE

HAHA!

WAL★MART

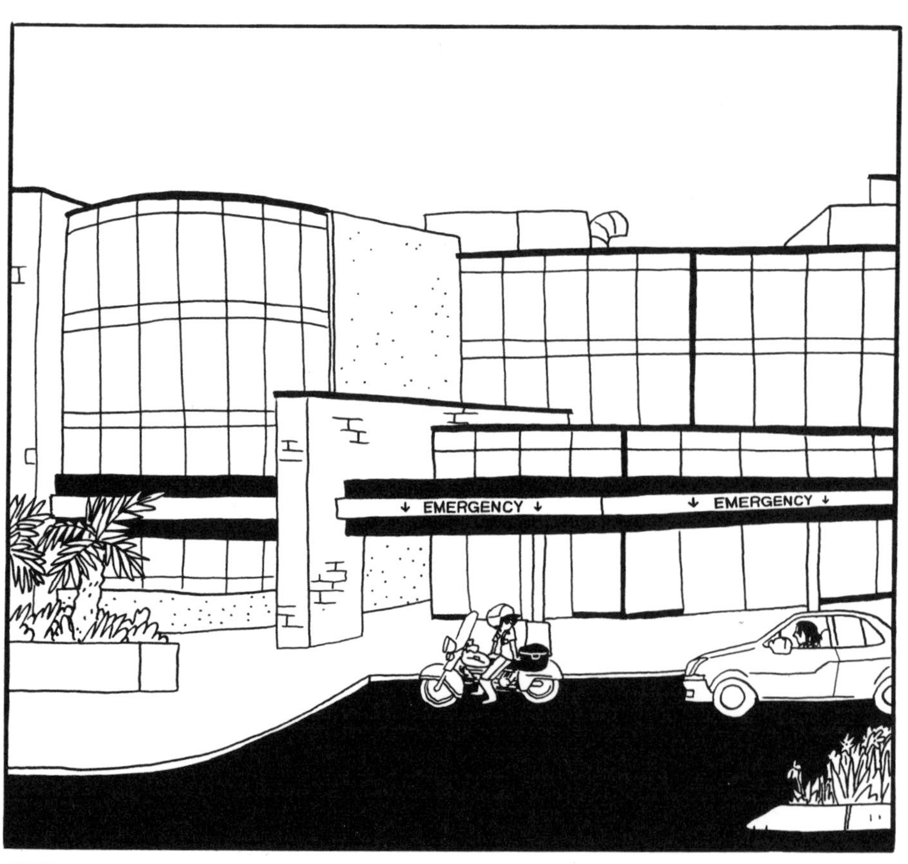
EMERGENCY
EMERGENCY

Fuck!
He's never going to give up!

Hold on, kiddo!

Doctor!
PAM

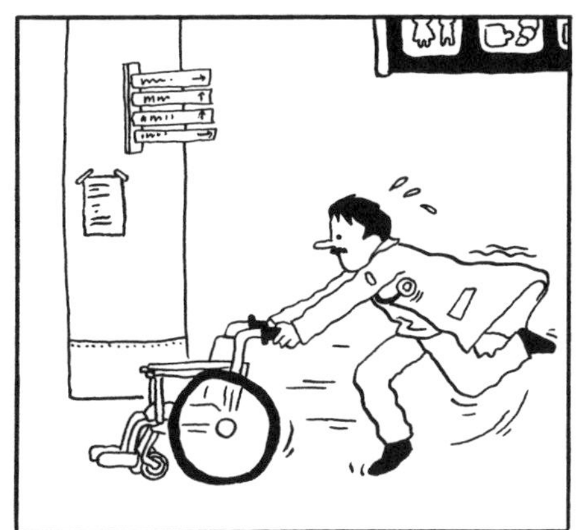

What's wrong?
Isn't it obvious? An asthma attack...

That? Asthma?!
Uh...

It's okay... I'm his mother. I'm here!
Thanks, officer.

You're welcome.
At your service...

Does he have asthma attacks often? It looks more like a minor panic attack to me...
Uh...

Ma'am?

Could you excuse us for a minute?
Um...
Sure...

Oops, sorry.

Oh... Sorry.
Have a good day...

Sorry! Wrong room!
Congrats!
SPOUK

Here we go...

I can't tell if that cop is gone...
What do you think he has?
Dunno... He doesn't look like he's in good shape, though.

There aren't any flowers in here... He must not have a lot of visitors...
Mmm... I hope so...
We'll stay here for a while. I don't want to run into the doctor or the cop in the hallway...
Eugene!
What? It's like his grandkid came over to visit...

Pfff... Whatever...

New developments in the multiple robberies reported in Prescott.
ORGANIZED CRIME

Last Saturday, the quiet town of Prescott was the target of a wave of multiple attacks...
Louder!

Banks, post offices, jewelry stores... 52 robberies on the same day, at the same time, and in the same town.

Taken by surprise, the police were not able to arrest any suspects.
But there were new developments in the case this morning when...

...the Chief of Police announced that they have uncovered the murdered bodies of several suspects. None of the stolen items were found at the crime scene.
...

The police have located 14 bodies, but also said they expect to find more in the coming days...

Traitors...

Uhh?!
Who would do that?! Huh?!
Who do you think they got?
Not Sofia, right?

I don't know, Kitty.

Scootch over...
What are we doing to do?

We lose the itinerary and we forget about the meeting point. The rest...
It'll be okay...

I'll go call Hank...
He might have more info about
what's going on...

Stay here.

Mom?

You're coming back,
right? Don't leave
me here...

Don't worry...
I'll never leave
you...

Eugene?

Eugene?

Kitty?
Here...

I talked to Hank and we're going...
TADAAA
Oh...
Haha
So?!

I also found something to bleach yours...

Will you do it?
Come on!
Okay.
Cool!!!

Doris
DINER
OPEN ALL NIGHT
SIMPLY THE
Best Coffee
OPEN
99¢
BUDWEISER
TRY THE
Doris Burger

Doris
DINER
Coffee?
No thanks...

It's so weird being blonde.
I think you look beautiful like that!
That's nice of you...
So?
What do we do now?

Not here...
Doris
DINE
MORD
NEW MURDERS

We're here.
Hank lives up there.
But we'll make our first stop at...

THE HOME DEPOT

And then a second stop around here.
There's nothing there.
Exactly.

Marker 634.
Bingo!
VT3
634
EDM409

Once we get there, I want you to remember every little detail.
Mhm.

Don't take too much. We'll come back for the rest...
Okay.

Where's north?
That way...

So, from marker 634, we walk 436 steps north...

...10, 11, 12, 13...

234, 235, 236, 237, 238...

435...
aaand 436!

Here, take this.
Put a mark on the three
nearest trees...
I'll go pick up the rest.
The knife is
for you.
It's a gift.
Cool!

Always keep it
with you.
You might
need it
soon...
CRRR

I think it's deep enough.

Come on.
Let's fill it up.

No last words?
Pff... Dummy!

It's weird, though.
Yeah, all of that for this...

Here, put that in your bag...
That's all?

You only kept that much?
That's 10 thousand dollars, Eugene. We can last months on that...

And when things calm down, maybe I'll be able to get a job.
Me too!

I think we're ready to go to Hank's...

Oh...
And don't tell him what we did here.
Safer that way...

Mom?

You trust Hank?

Try to sleep a bit.

Wake up.
We're here...

You all right, honey?
Mhm.
Freeze! Let me see those hands!

LET ME SEE THOSE HANDS!

Hank?
It's us.

May and Eugene.

May?

Dammit! What the fuck kept you? You should have been here hours ago!

It's nice to see you too, Hank...

He's sleeping?
Mhm.
MILK
So...
Still dragging your little bastard everywhere...
KCH.
Even on the run...
Fuck you, Hank. Give me a beer.
FRRRR
Did you learn anything?

Mmf...
Not much more than what you know...
Multiple robberies. Lots of money redistributed. Everybody goes their own way.
But you forgot about the "ambition" factor...
Some of them don't want to share. They also want control over that little wolf pack of criminals that you're in.
I know that...
Money and power, see...
Fuck, Hank! Who?!

Not sure...
WHO?!
I don't know, May.
I don't know...
They're bringing in the ones they find useful, good, and most of all, loyal...
But that doesn't seem to be the case for you and your bastard.
His name is Eugene!
PAF

We need to disappear, right?

Mhm.

I'll wake up Eugene.

Wait, May! Stay...

You're safe here.
Take a few days to rest...
We'll leave tomorrow.

I should have done what you did.

How could I buy into any solidarity between thieves?

Bah, it was a great heist.

Me...
I don't like people...
So that kind of
project...

Ooh, poor baby, he
doesn't like people...

RAAAAH
AAAH!

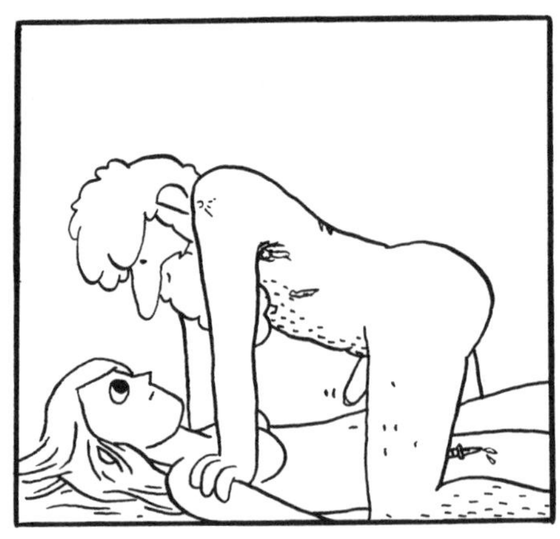

Mouahaha

Wait... Hush... Hush... Stop!
Fuck, STOP!

Mm?
THUMP

Come on, May...
Stop being so paranoid...
TAP TAP
We've got company...
Are you sure? I don't see anything.
I'm sure...

No way, no one's out there...
Tssss...

Who would come here? Huh?

Nobody would come for you here, May! Settle down...

Hank, get dressed and shut up!

Eugene, we need to...

I'm ready.

POC
TCHK
CHK

Still have your bike?

Mhm... Out back. Why? Do you want it?

You've got a car full of cash. What the fuck do you want to do with my ride?
You're crazy, May.

There isn't any money.

WHAT?!
What do you mean?!!

I don't have it anymore.
Fuck. I'm dead...

Shit, May, you never do anything right...

What the fuck did you do, Hank?

I... May, drop that gun.
It was to protect you...
I swear...

What did you do?!

The money for your life!!
Okay, I made a deal...
The money for your life...

I swear, May...

BLING

THUD

Our lives?
AAAH, okay, okay...

Aaaaah, take your foot off!
A third of the money against you.

I'm loaded in dept, May. I'm in deep shit and I...
You don't like people, I know...

PAM
CRACK

Rrrff... I... mmf...

SBAM

Mom?

MOM!

We need to leave...

Now!

Okay,
get up.
I need you to go to the back door and see if the path is clear, okay?
I'll be right there.
Mhm, okay.
Mmff. Fuck you're heavy, Hank...
Mmm...
FFFF
FFFFFFFFF

Okay, let's move...
Um.
HON A
Shit.
We take the car?

When I say "go," you run to the woods over there.
As fast as you can...

GO!

Hey, don't stop, come on!
Give me the bag...

BOOM

Haha...

I left them a little surprise for when they got into the house...
And Hank?

I don't know if he deserved it, but I made sure he was safe.

Let's keep moving...
FRR
FRR

What do we do now?

We stop the first car that doesn't seem to be driven by bad guys...

That's the plan?
Got a better idea?

No, no, it's perfect...

TAP

I hear an engine!

Is he sleeping?

Mhm.

BIG CHIEF ORANGE

Thanks, I don't know what we would have done without you.

Pfff, pleasure's mine.

It's true that it was an awkward place to do some hitchhiking.
What were you doing there, anyway?

Long story...

You're not very chatty, eh?

It's okay...
I can take care of that
part myself...

What do you
want me to
talk about?

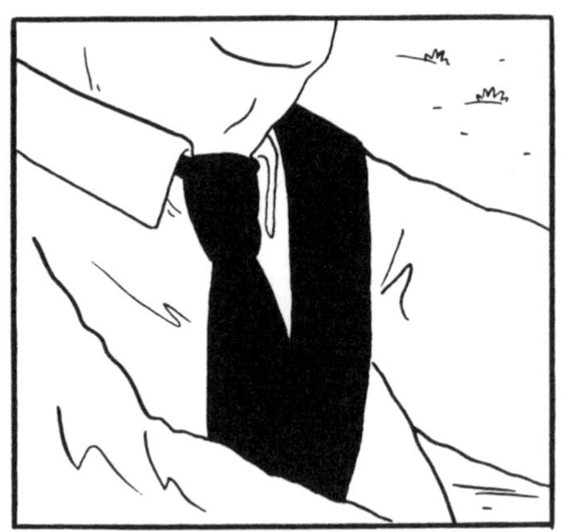

mmm...

A trucker with
a Gucci shirt
and a tie...

Why don't you
talk about that?

HAHA!

Haaa... Good one!
This'll take a few hours.

To explain my attire, we'll have to go back to when I used to work in Phoenix...
aloha

I was at one of those big financial companies.

Really?

I was 50 pounds heavier...
Slightly alcoholic...
...and a workaholic.

One day, I was staying late at the office...
Like I usually did...
SPEED CHECKED BY RADAR
50
STOP WHEN RED LIGHTS FLASH
GHOST TOWN
3

My boss told me to finish something that would have taken me all night.

But around 1 a.m., I was too drunk already and decided to head home.
Ouch...

So, I arrived home...

And BAM! Who's there with my wife?!
OCTO+
1

Not the boss?!

The boss!!!
PAM

He's fucking my wife on the kitchen counter.
OCTO+
UNLEADED
3.15 9
PHASE 7 Burrito's
SHOP
OCTO +
★ SHOP ★
And the worst part is, I hadn't even eaten yet!

I played the poor, resigned husband for weeks.
NUTS

My wife was going to ask me for a divorce, but I wanted a little time before that.

I put the house under my daughter's name and emptied all our accounts.
ICE

At work, I anonymously sent word of all the company's dirty business to the feds.

When my wife asked for the divorce, she didn't know that she wouldn't have any money and that her lover would soon be in jail...

Fuck man, I wouldn't want you as my enemy...

I wanted to see the country.
I was looking for a van, but ended up buying this truck.
BIG CHIEF ORANGE

That was 10 years ago.

And where does your clothing fit into all this?

That's just an old habit. I managed to change most things about my old life... But I still like the idea of wearing a tie to work.
Silly, right?

Haha...
Mhm.

You're not planning on robbing me with that gun of yours, eh?

No...
Of course not...

I can drop you off here?

Perfect.

Eugene... Hey...

Wake up, kitty...

Here's my card if you ever need a lift.

Augustus McCrae...

A trucker with old financial business cards...
Haha...

Here, go get us some food and drinks.

I'll try to find us a car.

We're not going to a motel?!

No. We need to keep moving...

What?! How long has it been since we last stopped?

I'm tired and dirty. I won't go, I'll stay here...

Sorry, Kitty...
We'll...

We could have kept on
doing fake checks.
BUT
NO!!

Mom wanted to
make a big hit!

One that would really
cover us and make us
normal people.

But we're not normal.
You're not a normal mom!

Just a shitty one.

BAF

We're still in the only city that's close to Hank's place! We're not hard to find.

Now go get us something to eat...

And then we're leaving this place and putting as much distance between us as them as we can.
Okay?!

And if you stink, buy some deodorant and a clean shirt...
Okay...

Eugene.

I'm sorry...
I know I'm not the best mom for you...
I thought I could give you more than what I had growing up.
I thought that if I loved you, it would be enough...
But I screwed it up...
MOM!!!

CRA

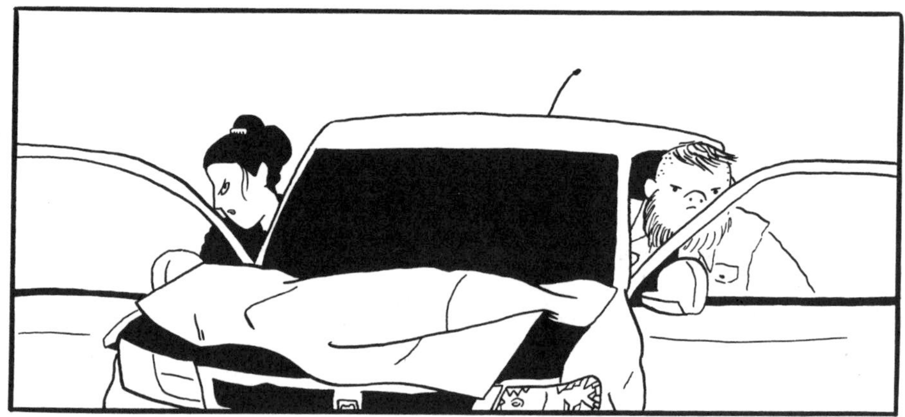

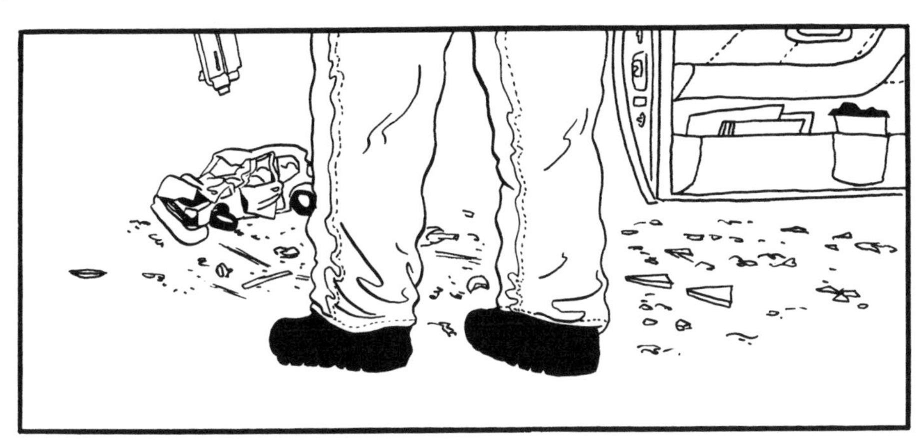

Bring May.

And the kid?
I don't care, do whatever you want...
Kill him...

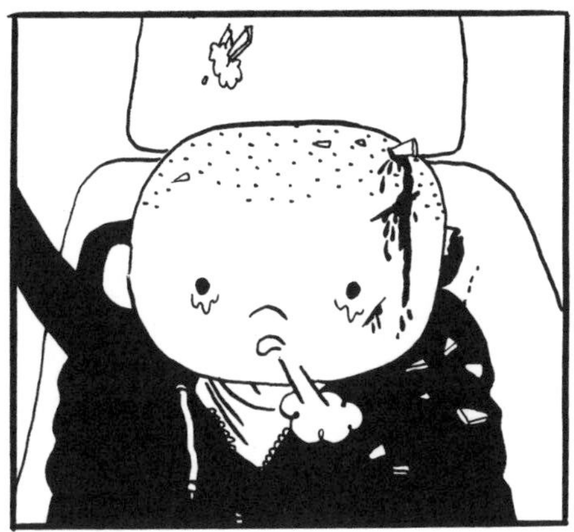

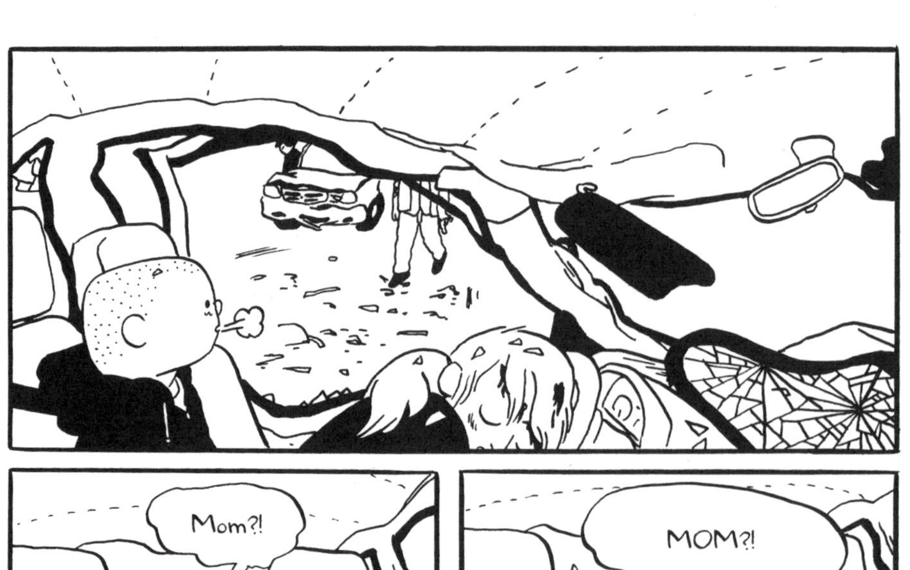

Mom?!

MOM?!

Humpf!
GRR

It's May that we want.

If you keep quiet, I'll let you live.

Mhm. Okay.

Ha!
You're a good little bastard.

FLITCH
SWOOSH

RAAAAH

Hahaha...

BLAM

Turn around, asshole!

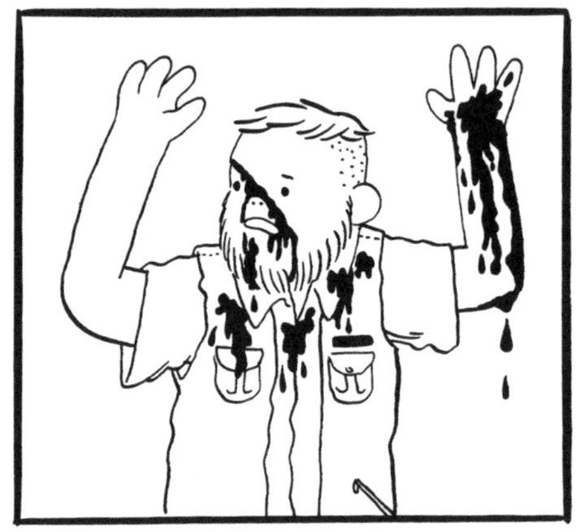

On your knees.
W... What?

Fuck...

Don't shoot, Lin!

BLAM
BLAM
BLAM

TING
TING
BLAM
BLAM

Move.

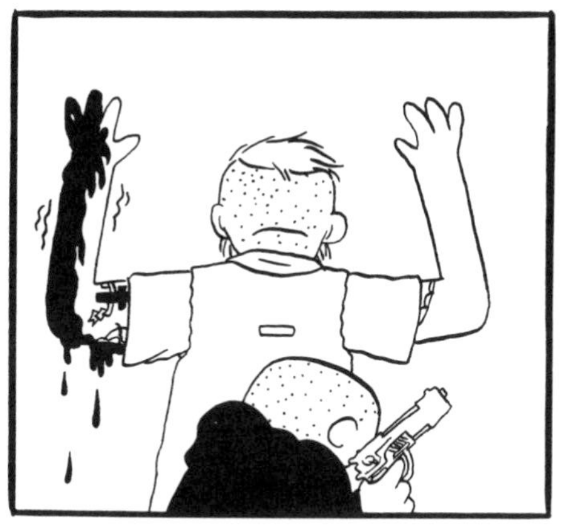

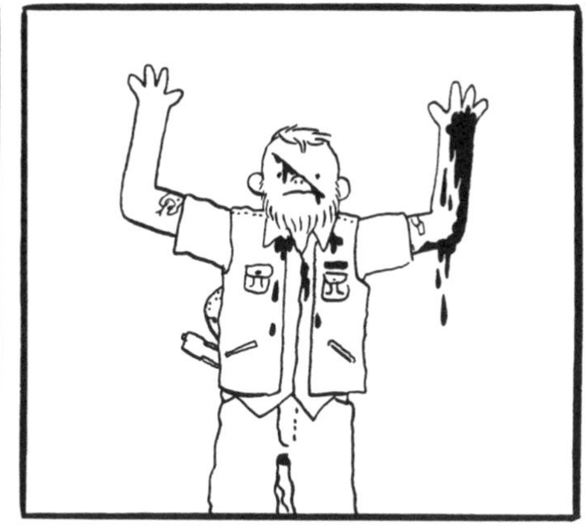

Fuck, Zwey...
Why're you so big!

Okay, okay... You win...
What do you want?!

Drop the gun!
Walk toward the desert!

Fucking kid.

CLICK

There.
Now what?

Go join Lin...

You better bring her somewhere quick. She'll bleed out if you don't.
I know.

Hey.
Fucking kid, right?
Mm.

VRRRRRRR

What did you expect? He was what, two years old, when she came with him in her arms?

Yeah, I guess when you are brought up in this life you learn to take care of yourself.
CRRR

There's a car coming...

Galaxy
Galaxy
Galaxy

Yes, in the back of the parking lot...

I don't know...
She's still unconscious.

No, she...

Mm...

They're coming!
Hurry!

Check the
parking lot...

AUTO+

POF

Okay?
Keep going...

FRRRRR

There!

That's our car...

They're gone...

I'll have a look inside.
Take a walk around.

BEER
POP
PEPSI
CHIPS

And?
Nothing.

They must have stolen a car and kept going.

What do we do now?

May is in bad shape, they won't get far...

Let's move on to the next town...

We'll find him at a doctor's or a hospital...
It might be good for you to see someone, too...
It's okay. I can wait. No worries.

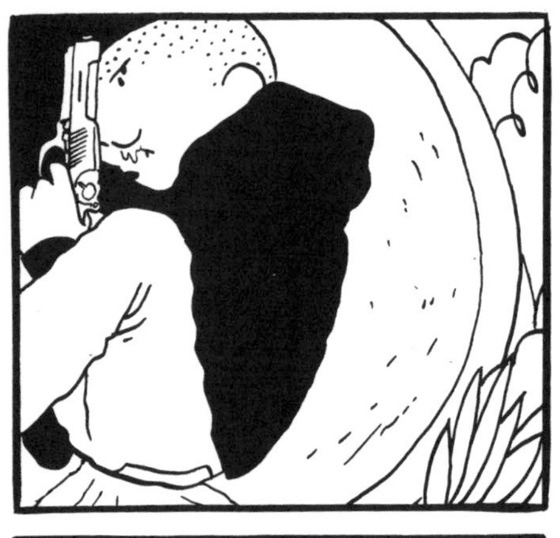

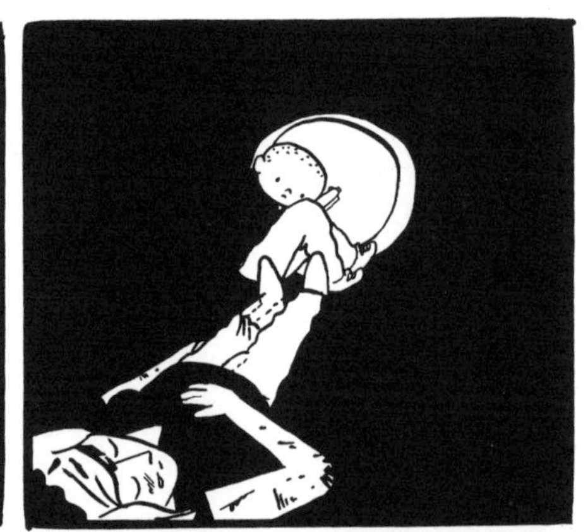

Eugene?

Eugene?!

Mama...

Hey Mark, could you go and find us some ice cream?
Yeah... Sure.

Be back in a sec...
ird...
ird...
Thanks, you're an angel...

May I sit?
aaa...

I was wondering when you'd finally come over and talk to me.
'gain...

You've been following my every step for weeks now.
BRRRR
aaaaa...

You a cop?
op.

No.
Ooop!

What the hell do you want, then?

You're doing well.

Four months now you've been able to move from one guy to the next...

From scam to scam...

A lot of people would have given up or gotten caught. Especially with a baby... But not you.

We both know...
May...

May and Eugene.
GENE!

We both know that you can't keep going on like this forever, May...

In the long run, it's just not bearable.

Who the fuck are you?!

A fucking Jehovah's Witness?! What do you want?!

I am interested in your skills.

And I can provide you with a roof over your head, money, independence...
Train you.

Train me?

Let's say that I'm part of a "group" that took our little scam to the next...
..."level."

What, you're kind of a Fagin character?

If we're talking English literature, I prefer Robin Hood.

If you're interested, you can find us at this address until the end of the week. After that...
...we're on the move.

Why would I be interested?

I wouldn't have gone through all this if I had any doubt you would be interested.

My name is Duane.

For the cab...

100 dollars?!

April...

Who was that guy?

Just a guy...
He was looking for
Castro Street...
Oh...Okay.

Nose.

PLAINS INDIAN ART
Phillies

She's still out...

We're almost there.

She's going to be okay.

Don't worry...

You did good by calling me...
I'm not a gangster, but I have some friends that will be able to help.

FRITZ the CAT

Welcome, May.

Here we are...

NATIVE at Taos Museum
...

hmff

May?

MOM!

MOM!!!

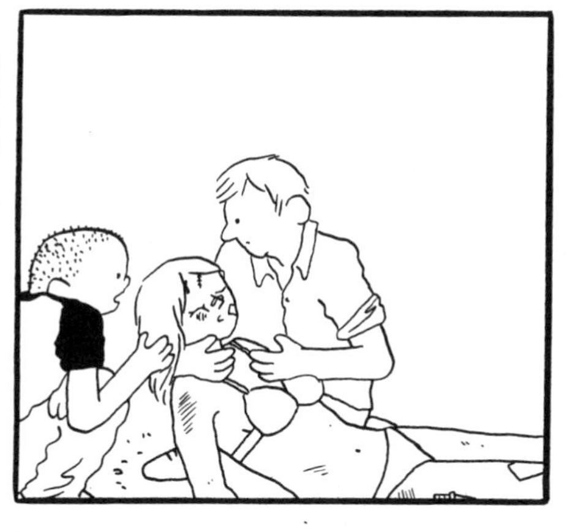

Feeling better?
Where... Where are... W...
...
You're at Achak and Numees' in north New Mexico.
My truck broke down in the area years ago...
They took me in for a night and I stayed four months...

We... Eugene and me, we...
We're in the middle of nowhere and they're like family, you don't have anything to fear here...
Eugene told me everything.
What happened?
What do you remember?
You dropped us off. We "borrowed" a car... And... That's it...
So... After I dropped you off...

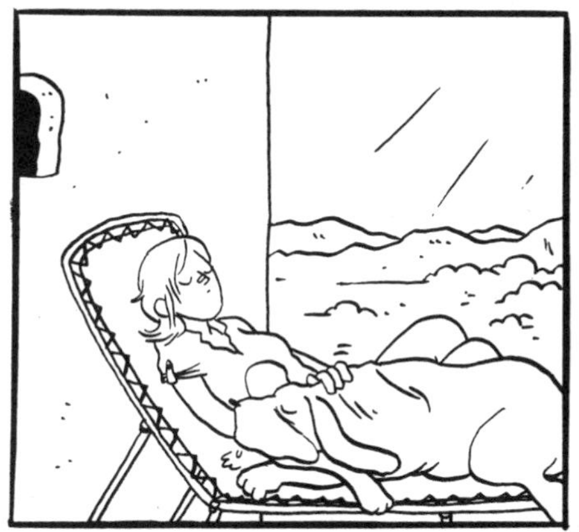

What are you doing?
Achak told me that if I could fix it, I could use it...

You're planning on leaving?
Mhm.

I need to gather some new information on our situation... Nothing risky...

Okay.
But leave Eugene here... He's just a kid...

Are you trying to protect him or just making sure I come back?
Pff...

She fixed the car.

I know.

And you're going to let her go?
Well, yeah...

Pff...

She just wants to gather information... Nothing too risky...

Pfff... You don't understand anything about that woman... Or organized crime...
RRRRRRR

I'll be back in about a week...

I need to figure all of this out...

I want to come with you.
Not this time, Kitty.

But I'll be careful... Promise...

It'll be all right.

RRRRRR

POC
POC
POC

Dinner's ready!
Umf.

You okay, Eugene?

It's already been four days since she left...

She knows what she's doing. Don't worry...

Don't worry?! If I hadn't been there the last time...

...she would be dead by now!
KHHH
KHHHH

FSHHH

She just wants to find a way to get you out of this bad situation without making too many waves...
Is that what she told you?

Mhm, nothing irresponsible...

FSHHH
Haha...

FSHHH
You really don't know her...

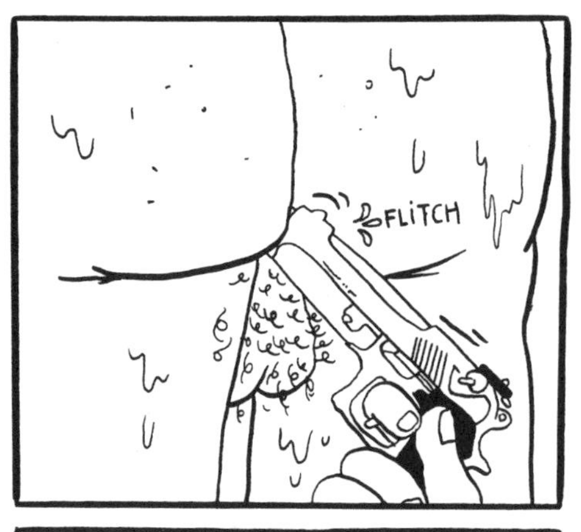
FLITCH

You?!
Hi, Zwey.

Come on... There's nothing to worry about.
Let's go and eat.

I can't concentrate with that barbecue smell, anyway...
Mm.

KNOCK KNOCK

Ah!
CRACK
KNOCK KNOCK
LIVE
Zwey?
HFF HFF
Open up, for fuck's sake!
Ugh.
PAK
Zwey! Open that fucking door!
Rrffl...
mgnnnnn...
mmmmm

PAC

PAC
PAC
PAC
PAC
PAC
PAC
PAC
PAC

Zwey?!
Fuck...
BAM
BAM

SBLAF
Zwey? Where are you?

Is it okay if I put hot chiles in your burger?
Mm!
KIPS

Zwey?

Zw...
SBAM

RAAAAH!

You?!

AAAAAH

TAP
TAP
TAP

PAM

PLOUF
PAF

You like it?
Best burger ever! Could I have a second one?

Eat this one first, kid...

FSHHH
LIVE FAST

He's starting to get worried about his mother.

And you're not?

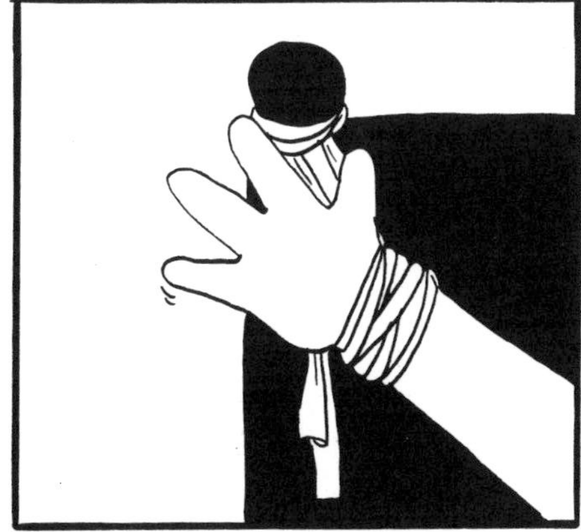

mmm...

Shhh...

We need to talk...

Where's Lin?

Lin can't help you right now...

Come on, May... Please. We're old friends...

Good...
Slowly...

Put it in
the bag.

EUGENE!
Whoa!
Hey!

Your mom's on
the phone!

KSSS

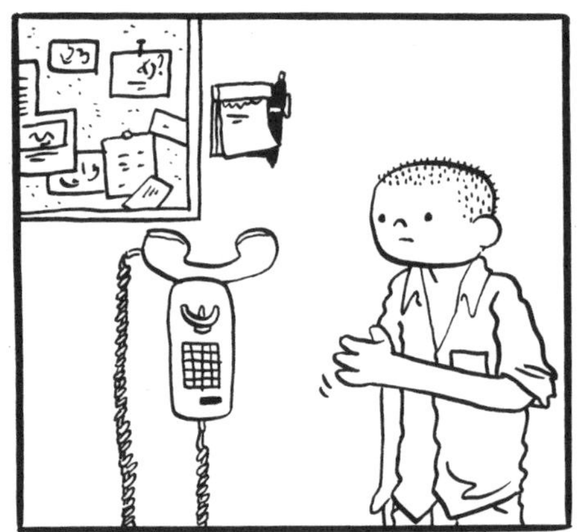

Hello?

Hey! Kitty!
How are you?
SECOND HAND BOOK SHELTER

Mom?!

I'm sorry I left, Kitty...
But everything is fine... Don't worry...

Of course I'm okay...
I found...

Lin and Zwey?!
What are you going to do?

Oh...

WHAT?!

You can't trust him!!!

Don't worry...
Zwey only serves his best interests. And right now, his best interest is me...

Duane is the one behind all this...
The multiple robberies were just excuses to round up the best thieves on the West Coast.
He chose the most talented and tried to get rid of the others.
He thinks he's like the "King of Thieves."
But thanks to Zwey, I've got the list of people that didn't make the cut and are still alive.
Like us?
Yeah, like us...

Sofia is on that list.
Lin and Zwey were after her, so we should find her right away...
Cool!
So, what's the plan?
When do you come to pick me up?
The plan is I don't come and pick you up.
What?

Listen, we can't stay hiding like this forever.

I'm going to bring some of these "undesirables" on that list together and then bring down Duane.

But...
I...

...

Leave him alone.

I don't understand, Mom. What about me?

I think it's time for you to go back...
Wh... What?!
Where?
You still have that knife I gave you?
The handle unscrews...
Can't I wait for you here?
No.
I'll join you later.
I'm really sorry.
Everything I did was for your own good...
I love you, Kitty.

ANDERSEN
615 Taylor Ave
Alameda - CA
sorry...

Come for a ride, kid.

Need help?
I'll manage this time...

You think you can also manage to keep up?

USA

TUUUT TUUU
It's time...
Mhm.
SAN FRANCISCO

Will you be okay?
Mhm.

I don't know what awaits you over there, but if you don't like it... You're always welcome here...

Always. Okay?
Mhm.

I'll try to watch over your mom, if she lets me...

KTCH

KFC

MIDDLESEX

ROY'S
GAS
CAFE

Kid...
We're here.

U-HAUL

ANDERSEN

Yes?

Can I help you?
Um... is Mr. Andersen here?
Who are you?
Um...
I got his address through... Um... His...
Well...
I'm his...
Um... It's a bit complicated, actually...
I would rather speak to him face to face...

I think that... Well, I'm not sure, but...
It's possible that I could be his...
Eugene?
Is that you?
...
It's you!
615

CRASH

CRACK

When he died, I was sure you would come back.

And April?

Where is she?

Um...

Where is your sister?

DRIIIIIIIIIIIIIIING
ENCINAL HIGH SCHOOL

GOJE
BULLS
23

Eugene?

Wanna come play Assassin's Creed at Tim's with us?
Thanks, but...

...Not today. Sorry.
Okay... Too bad. See you tomorrow.

yum yum
COMAN
BUFFALO BUR
Augustus!
Hey, kid!

You have time to take a walk with me?
Mhm.

So, how's it going here?
Er...

She... she's not my mother.

April... I mean, May to you. She's not my mom...

She's my sister.

I'm staying at Jacky's. She's my mother.

My dad died a few months ago...
BOOKS
BOOKS
478
OPEN

She must have known or she would have never sent me here...

He was violent. With Jacky, mostly. Mom, um... April stood up to him.

When he started abusing me, it was too much for April.

She ran away with me under her arm. She was 16 and I just turned one.

A teenager alone with a baby... It must have just been easier to say that she was your mother...
Mhm.
And in time, she became...

She rang Duane's doorbell and that's when shit got serious...
Well, he won't be bothering you anymore...

What?
Blam.

No more Duane or his gang?
No more Duane, but the gang...

...There's been a change in leadership.
Who?

Sophie... And your mother.

You've seen her?

Yeah, just before coming here.

She's in prison in Minnesota under the name June Carson.

Small charges, 18 months.
They couldn't connect her to Duane or the robberies.

Will she come back for me once she's out?

Of course she'll come and see you...

I'm not sure if I'll be able to see her or write to her there... Will you tell her something for me?
Sure.

Tell her that she'll always be my mom.

BIRD SANCTUARY
NO TRESPASSING

What did you tell Jacky about your life before all this?

I told her we lived in a hippie commune in New Mexico...

Haha, and she believed you?
Haha, yeah...

Haha!
The Rainbow Connection Commune on Sunshine Farm de la Joya Pueblo.
PFFF...

Neither of you could even pretend to be hippies...
TAP

Yeah, hippies that rob banks...

BURRI
BACO

615

Everything all right?
I broke my key in the lock...

I'm waiting for the locksmith.

615

615
CHK CHK
CHK
CLACK

It's open!

The hippies taught you that?

Haha, no! April is always distracted. Her home and car keys would disappear pretty regularly. It started to be too much money to call the locksmith each time... So I learned...
Ah.

Come and help me with the groceries.
I bought stuff to make pizzas. You like those?
Yummy.

OLIVE

LINO
LINO
50177
LINO